"Do you see that?"

Jimmy exclaimed. "He's monkeying with those gumball machines."

"He's up to something," T.J. said. "Something sneaky."

"Something underhanded," added Dottie.

"Something crooked," Jay concluded with a nod. "I bet he just retrieved another stolen diamond from one of those gumball machines."

"Sure," said T.J. "And now he's going into the store to pass it on to his accomplice. Come on, let's shadow him."

THE CASE OF
The Gumball Bandits

·

William Alexander

·

Troll Associates

Cover art: Judith Sutton
Illustrated by: Dave Henderson

Library of Congress Cataloging-in-Publication Data

Alexander, William, (date)
    The case of the gumball bandits / by William Alexander.
        p.   cm.—(The Clues Kids; #3)
    Summary: The Clues Kids, five foster children living with Chief
Klink and his wife, suspect that jewel thieves are stashing their
diamonds in gumball machines.
    ISBN 0-8167-1696-X (lib. bdg.)   ISBN 0-8167-1697-8 (pbk.)
    [1. Mystery and detective stories. 2. Foster home care—Fiction.]
I. Title. II. Series: Alexander, William. The Clues Kids; #3.
PZ7.A3786Cau 1990
[Fic]—dc20   89-36558

A TROLL BOOK, published by Troll Associates

JAY LOCKE

<u>Code name:</u> Clicker—Jay takes the pictures...lots of pictures. No clue escapes his lens because he shoots everything—windows, pets, doorknobs, lint—everything.

T.J. BOOKER

<u>Code name:</u> Smoke Screen—T.J. is the greatest disguise artist in the world (he asked me to say that). Actually, he *does* make up some great disguises. Some of them are pretty strange...but that's T.J.

JIMMY LOCKE

<u>Code name:</u> Jaws—He's the information man. He asks the questions. With his razor-sharp mind (he *made* me say that), Jimmy can break down any suspect.

DOTTIE BREWSTER

<u>Code name:</u> Short Stuff—She's the normal one of the bunch. Dottie looks for clues, tails crooks, keeps track of their fees, and tries to keep the others out of trouble. That's harder than you think!

LEE VAN THO

<u>Code name:</u> Smudge—Lee gets the fingerprints. He really gets the fingerprints. He usually makes a mess getting the prints, but he gets them!

C·H·A·P·T·E·R
1

*T*his is Dozerville, Illinois, population 12,533 and one half. The half citizenship is the proud possession of Boswell Noteworthy, a chimpanzee.

Boswell is the pet of the town's census taker. He gets to attend town meetings, march in the annual Dozerville Mule and Plow Day Parade, and mow the lawn in front of the mayor's house. But that's another story.

This tale is about gumballs, thieves, deception, and—the Clues Kids.

"Uh-oh," twelve-year-old Jay Locke said. "Cosmic Cop has had it this time. Hot Rocks has him trapped on that runaway asteroid. He'll never get off alive." He stood up and clicked off the TV.

Jimmy, Jay's twin brother, pulled a notebook from his shirt pocket and thumbed to a page near the middle. "Sure he will," he replied. "My records show that Cosmic Cop always gets out of traps in two episodes or less."

"And into another one right afterwards," added Lee Van Tho, their half-Vietnamese foster brother.

Cosmic Cop was the kids' favorite cartoon character, an intergalactic detective who always caught his alien. So far.

Jay shook his head. "Other traps, maybe," he said with a sigh. "But an asteroid plunging at the speed of light into a white dwarf star? This time it's really curtains for Cosmic."

Jay went back to the couch and plopped down on a big purple pillow. The pillow gave a shout and shoved him off the couch. He landed with a thump.

"What—!" Jay sprang, then made a grab for the pillow. Suddenly two sneakers appeared at one end of the pillow, and the grinning face of a thin black boy at the other end.

"Some disguise, huh?" the boy demanded. "I fooled you, didn't I?" He struggled out of the big purple pillowcase. This was T.J. Booker, ten years old and the fourth member of the group.

"I knew you were there all along," a voice said from the corner. Dottie Brewster stood up, stretched, and pushed her long, curly red hair back behind her ears. She was only eight, the youngest of the family, but she *noticed* things. She didn't let the others forget it, either.

"Come on," Jay said. "Let's go to the clubhouse. We have to make some plans."

The house was an old one, with three floors, loads of rooms, and a shadowy, dusty attic. Attached to one side was what used to be the barn. Now it was the garage, workshop, tool shed, and second home to their basset hound, Snoop, when he got into trouble. That didn't usually happen more than three days out of the week.

At the back, up a steep ladder, was the hayloft. All the hay was long gone, eaten up by horses that were long gone, too. But the kids had filled the room up again in their own style. They had built a desk out of stacked milk crates and an old door. Some old chairs and big pillows gave them places to relax. And then there was all their professional equipment—binoculars, cameras, disguises, leaky cans of fingerprint powder, and a lot of other stuff that was sure to be useful someday.

A sign on the wall, hand-lettered by Lee, said, ****CLueS KiDS— Wold Headquarters****. Jay had wanted to pencil in the missing r, but the others felt it gave the place a homey touch.

Jimmy sat down in an old green kitchen chair and tilted onto the back legs. The chair swayed and let out a screech of protest. Jimmy grabbed the top of the desk and sat up straight again.

"We've got four whole days off," he said. "And nothing to do with them."

"We could read," Dottie suggested.

Jimmy gave Dottie a dirty look. "Like I said—we don't have anything to do."

Jay was sitting on a big pillow, hugging his knees. "Smashing a criminal empire would be fun," he said. "Or maybe crushing some super genius's plot to rule the world. Yeah, we could do that in four days."

T.J. smiled. "What you want is a case to solve."

Jay put his hands behind his head. "Isn't that what I said?"

Lee was busy dusting a recent issue of *Kid Detective* with fingerprint powder. He looked up and said, "Come on, Jay. Didn't we find Brad Dribble's basketball when he lost it?"

"Sure," Jay said with a snort. "It was stuck in the hoop. All we had to do was go out in his yard and look."

"What about Penny Fay Flier's lost gym shoes?" demanded T.J. "Finding them wasn't so easy, was it?"

Jay grinned. "Not until we figured out that she'd thrown them in the washer with a new pair of jeans," he replied.

"I told you those blue sneakers were an important clue," Dottie said quietly.

T.J. threw a pillow at her.

Lee said, "Well, what about the time when Shelly Anodour's pet skunk got loose?"

"I never want to hear about that skunk again," Dottie proclaimed. "The whole case smelled. Anyway, Jay's right. We haven't had a real case since the Ghost of Shockly Manor. We've got to do something."

"We could put up posters," said Jimmy. *"Crooks and Spies Wanted—Apply at Dozerville Police Station."*

"Why would a crook want to go to a police station?" Lee asked. "It isn't logical."

"It isn't serious, either," Jimmy replied. "Anyway, the police would never tell *us* about it, even if some nutty crooks did show up. They haven't even asked us to help them catch that pickpocket."

"The one who's been hitting all the stores downtown, you mean?" asked Dottie. She frowned. "I know—why don't we try to catch him ourselves?"

T.J. jumped up. "Sure!" he exclaimed. "I could disguise myself as a big purse. The minute the bad guy tried to take my wallet, *bam!* I'd grab him."

"I don't think—" Jay began.

"Hey, kids," a voice called from the garage. "Are you up there?"

They crowded into the doorway. Phil Klink, their foster father, was looking up at them. He was a tall, heavyset man in his late fifties. He had wavy, white hair and a bushy white moustache and beard. Until his retirement, he had been Dozerville's chief of police. Even now the police still called on him for helpful tips.

"How are you doing?" Phil asked. "Having fun?"

Jay spoke for them all. "Sure, Chief," he said. "We're fine."

"Good. I'm going to run a few errands. Then I have to pick up Patty when her committee meeting is finished. We should be home in an hour or so."

Patty, the children's foster mother, was one of the most active members of the community board. She usually seemed to be on her way to or from a meeting to do something to better the town. But she always managed to find time for the kids.

Phil climbed into his proudest possession, a forty-year-old station wagon with a real wood body and real leather seats, then leaned out the window to say, "Don't get into any trouble."

"Sure thing," Jay replied.

"You bet," added T.J.

The others just smiled and waved. As soon as the car backed out, they turned and looked at Jay.

"It's all right," Jay said weakly. "I just said that we wouldn't get into trouble. I didn't say what we would do if trouble found us."

"I think it just did," said Jimmy, looking at the open door of the garage.

Everyone turned and looked. Laurie Peters, a girl from T.J.'s class, was standing there. As usual, she looked as if she had just stepped out of a store window downtown. Not a hardware store, either—an exclusive kids' clothing store.

"Hi, guys," she called. "Hello, T.J."

"Hi, Laurie, what's up?" T.J. replied.

She giggled. "You are!" Then her face turned serious. "Can I come up, too?" she asked. "I want to talk to you. I need your help."

"I bet she lost a barrette," Dottie muttered to Jimmy. He shushed her. Laurie climbed up to the loft and followed them into the clubhouse.

"Okay, Laurie," Jay said, once they were all settled down. "What's the problem?"

"You've got to save me!" Laurie cried, flinging her hands up in the air. "I don't know where else to turn!"

"Try turning right or left," muttered Dottie. Jimmy poked her in the ribs, then smiled at Laurie.

"We'll be glad to save you," he said. "But what do you want us to save you for? I mean, from?"

Laurie looked at him with wide eyes. "There's a gang of crooks after me," she declared. "One of them was following me before."

T.J. said, "If you thought somebody was following you, you should have told a police officer."

"But I couldn't," Laurie wailed. "I was afraid to. I think the police are after me, too! You'll help me, won't you?"

"You've come to the right place, ma'am," Jay said. "The Clues Kids Detective Agency—we detect clues. But we can't help you unless we have all the facts."

Dottie couldn't keep quiet any longer. "Yeah," she said. "Like, to start with, why should anybody, cops or crooks, be after you?"

Laurie looked around the circle. "You won't tell, will you?" she said. "Cross your heart? And pledge on your most secret pledge of honor and truth?"

The kids sighed. They all made silly signs with their hands, crossed their eyes, and kissed various lucky charms they carried. "We pledge," they said in unison.

Laurie reached into her school bag and pulled out something wrapped in a blue ban-

danna. She carefully untied the knots, then held out her hand.

"I think it has something to do with this," she said softly. There in her palm, sparkling and flashing, was the biggest, brightest diamond the kids had ever seen.

C·H·A·P·T·E·R
2

Jimmy let out a loud whistle. He liked the effect so much that he did it again.

"Wow," said T.J. "What a rock!"

Jay grabbed his camera and took a closeup shot of Laurie's hand and the diamond.

Even Dottie took a closer look, then said, "That's amazing. Where did you get it, Laurie?"

"That's the most amazing part," Laurie said. "You know those gumball machines in front of Toots' Sweets, the candy store?"

"Oh, no," groaned Lee. He rolled his eyes and stared at the ceiling. "No!"

Laurie looked puzzled. "You don't? Why not? They've been there forever and ever. You put in your money and you get out a gumball, or a little toy, or something like that. You must have seen them."

Jay stepped in. "I think Lee said 'Oh, no' because he guessed what was coming next."

"Really?" Laurie looked even more puzzled. "I don't know how he could have. I mean, how could anyone guess that I'd get a real diamond out of a gumball machine?"

"I must have ESP," said Lee.

"Anyway, how do you know it's real?" Dottie demanded.

Laurie wrinkled her forehead. "I don't *know* it's real," she replied, "but just look at it!" She moved her hand a little, and the stone sent flashes of light around the room. "Doesn't it *look* real?"

"It sure does," said Jay. "But they do some amazing things with plastic these days."

Lee reached out his hand. "Can I see it for a minute, Laurie?" he asked. "I'll give it right back." He picked up the glittering stone and walked over to the old mirror on the wall.

"What are you going to do?" Laurie said. "Don't—!"

Lee scraped the stone across the surface of the mirror. The noise was awful, much worse than fingernails on a blackboard. Laurie clapped her hands over her ears.

Lee leaned close to the mirror and looked at the result. He let out a whistle of his own. "Take a look at that," he said to the others.

"It scratched the glass . . . just the way a real diamond would."

Everyone crowded around the mirror to look at the line scratched across it. Then T.J. said, "But if the diamond is real . . . then so is the danger!"

"Of course it's real," Laurie said. "That's why you've got to help me. The diamond must be stolen, and the crooks want to get it back from me. That's why they're following me. And I can't just turn it over to the police. What if it *is* stolen? They'll probably think *I* did it."

"They won't believe you found it in a gumball machine, that's for sure," said Dottie.

Jay sat down at the desk and leaned back. The chair gave a loud creak. "What does it mean?"

"It means the chair is going to break," T.J. replied.

"Not that, silly—the gumball machine! What was a diamond doing in a gumball machine?"

T.J. scratched his chin. "Pretending to be a gumball?" he suggested.

"Somebody hid it there," Jimmy said. "Let's say it was stolen, and the thief worked in a gumball factory, and the cops were about to search him. So he—"

"Hid the diamond in with the gumballs,"

Lee shouted. "Sherlock Holmes had a case just like that, where the thief hid a stolen jewel inside a Christmas goose."

"That's a silly thing to do," Dottie scoffed. "How would he ever get it back?"

Jimmy grinned. "Yeah, I guess his goose was cooked!"

The others booed, and T.J. threw a pillow at Jimmy, who threw it back. A war seemed about to break out, but Jay took charge.

"Dottie has a good point," he said. "Why would the thieves put the diamond someplace where they couldn't get it back?"

Dottie said, "What if they didn't *want* to get it back? Remember on *Cosmic Cop*, when Hot Rocks stole the emerald necklace of Princess Verdigris and stashed it in that abandoned space station?"

"That's right," Lee said excitedly. "He left it there for his accomplices to pick up, but Cosmic Cop got there first."

Jimmy nodded. "Then the jewel thieves must have put the diamond in the gumball machine on purpose," he said. "It was waiting there for somebody."

"You mean, like a fence?" asked Lee. "Someone who was going to buy it from the thieves? Sure, that makes fence. I mean, sense. And then Laurie came along and got the diamond before the fence could get it."

"He must have been pretty mad when he found out," T.J. said.

"He must have spent a lot of money on gumballs, too," Jimmy added. "Hey, that's right—if we want to catch the fence, all we have to do is find out who was hanging around, buying tons of gumballs."

Lee jumped up. "Come on," he said, grabbing his portable fingerprinting set. "I bet he left prints all over the gumball machine. We'll have him in no time!"

Toots' Sweets was in the middle of the block. It was next door to Appleton's Fruits and Vegetable Stand, and two doors down from a pizza shop. In Dozerville, almost everything is two doors down from a pizza shop.

As the kids stopped for a moment to inhale the aroma of mozzarella and pepperoni, the door of the candy store opened. A man walked out—a very large man, especially around the middle. He was wearing a light-colored suit and white shoes, and he had a cane in one hand.

He paused in the doorway, looked back, and said, "I can see you're a woman who knows her business, Miss Kossmeyer. I like a woman who knows her business."

He chuckled, making several of his chins shake, and turned to go. When he saw the little cluster of kids watching him, his eyes narrowed. For a moment, he looked really mean. Then he smiled and chuckled again. "Good day," he said to them, and waved his cane. "Good day!"

"Wow. *Who* was *that*?" Lee demanded as soon as the large man was out of sight.

"I don't know," T.J. replied, "but he's sure got the build to play Santa Claus."

Jimmy gave a snort. "The build, maybe, but Santa is supposed to go 'Ho, ho, ho,' *not* 'Heh, heh, heh!' "

Jay tugged at his earlobe. This was a sure sign that he was thinking hard. "You know," he said slowly, "I have a feeling I've seen that fat man before."

"Sure," said Jimmy. "In the 'Before' part of a diet ad."

Jay shook his head. "No, it was ... Oh, never mind. Let's get on with our investigation. Laurie, why don't you show us exactly what you did before."

"For sure," Laurie said with a smile. She seemed to like being the center of attention. She stepped over to the gumball machines. "I just took out my money and put it ... Oh! That's silly!"

All of them crowded around. "What's wrong?" Jay demanded.

Laurie frowned, "There's tape over the coin

slot, and a little sign saying 'Out of Order'. But it wasn't out of order before."

"You're sure this is the right machine?" asked Lee, reaching into his bag. He took out a bottle of fingerprint powder and a very dusty paintbrush.

"Of course I am," Laurie replied. "I remember it was the one in the middle. And now it isn't working. How funny!"

"You know what's even funnier?" observed Dottie. "There are usually only two gumball machines out here—those two on each end. So the one where you got the, uh, the *object*, is not only broken, it's brand new!"

While Jay took a photo of the broken gumball machine, his twin brother nodded wisely and said, "Very strange, Dottie, very strange. I think we ought to ask Miss Kossmeyer a few questions."

"And I think we ought to try the machines that *are* working," T.J. said. "Who knows what we'll get from them? Hey, who's got some change? Dottie?"

Dottie backed away. "Sorry, T.J.," she said quickly. "I'm broke."

"I'll be right back," Jimmy said, opening the door to the candy store.

"I'll come, too," called Lee. "Just a second." He quickly blew the fingerprint powder off the gumball machine. A lot of it ended up on his cheeks and nose. He brushed his face with his arm, making a big smudge on the sleeve of his shirt. He started to rub at that with his other hand, then shrugged and left it alone.

From behind the counter, Miss Tootsie Kossmeyer said, "Hi, kids. What can I do for you?"

Jimmy took out one of the Clues Kids business cards that T.J. had designed and handed it to her. She looked at it and raised her eyebrows.

"Do you mind if we ask you a few questions?" said Jimmy. "We're just trying to get some facts, ma'am."

"Sure, go ahead," the candy store owner replied. She sounded as if she wanted to laugh. "What about?"

"We're doing a school project, kind of a survey," Jimmy explained. "It's about whether people would rather spend their money on candy or gum or little prizes. And we noticed that you have three gumball machines out on the sidewalk. Do people put a lot of money into them?"

"I guess you could say that," Miss Kossmeyer said.

"Anyone in particular? I mean, have you noticed someone putting a lot of money into them?"

The woman shook her head. "Not really," she said.

"Oh." Jimmy hesitated. He glanced over at Lee for help.

"Gee," Lee said. "That's very interesting. Uh, didn't you used to have just two gumball machines?"

"That's right."

Lee glanced out the window. "But there are three out there now," he pointed out.

"That's right," Miss Kossmeyer said again.

Jimmy cut in. "And one of them is out of order."

"You don't say?" This time the woman laughed aloud. "I'll have to do something about that, won't I?"

Meanwhile, out on the sidewalk, T.J. was showing Jay and Laurie all the loot he had gotten from the two machines. Aside from a month's supply of gumballs, there was a tiny harmonica, four rings in different colors, a braided bracelet, a "Smile!" button with a broken clasp, a green plastic Scottie dog half an inch long, and an orange plastic shovel and pail, also half an inch long.

"No diamonds?" Jay demanded.

"Not a single one," T.J. replied. "And all of us are out of money, too. Dottie, you don't—?"

Dottie turned away and pretended not to hear. Across the street, a skinny teenager was leaning against the front of Glover's Department Store. What caught her eye was his maroon jacket with yellow sleeves. Yellow letters across the front spelled out "JUNIOR."

"Hey, guys," Dottie said, "what school's colors are maroon and yellow?"

"Beats me," Jay replied. "Why?"

Dottie shrugged and said, "There's a guy wearing them across the street, that's all. I think he's looking at us. It says 'JUNIOR' on his jacket. What does that mean? Junior high, or what?"

Laurie froze. "Maroon and yellow?" she gasped. "Junior? But that's him! That's the guy who was following me! The one who's after the diamond!"

C·H·A·P·T·E·R
3

"*I*'m sure that's him,"
Laurie insisted. "He's the one who's been
following me!"

Dottie, Jay, and T.J. turned to stare at the
teen in the yellow and maroon jacket. He
noticed them looking at him and turned his
back.

"Do you see that?" Jay exclaimed. "He's
monkeying with those gumball machines."

"*More* gumball machines?" T.J. said. He
looked down at his handful of plastic novelties and brightly-colored gumballs. "Hey, what
do I do with all this stuff?"

"Stick it in your school bag," Dottie replied.

"I can't, it's full of disguises." He raised
the flap and peered inside. "Well, *mostly* full."
He dropped the gumballs and tiny toys inside.

"I've seen that guy all over," Laurie was

explaining to Jay. "My mom takes me shopping a lot, so I'll have enough clothes for school, you know?"

"She's already got enough clothes for a whole classroom," Dottie whispered to T.J.

Laurie didn't seem to hear. "And shopping is such hard work," she continued. "You have to walk all over town, and look at things, and try them on. It's really exhausting—physically and emotionally exhausting."

T.J. put his mouth near Dottie's ear. "I'll bet her mom says that all the time," he said with a laugh.

Dottie just shrugged.

"What's he doing now?" Jay said. Across the street, the guy in the two-tone jacket suddenly stopped fiddling with the gumball machines and straightened up. He gave a quick glance up and down the sidewalk, then slipped into the department store.

"He's up to something," T.J. said. "Something sneaky."

"Something underhanded," added Dottie.

"Something crooked," Jay concluded with a nod. "I bet he just retrieved another stolen diamond from one of those gumball machines."

"Sure," said T.J. "And now he's going into the store to pass it on to his accomplice. Come on, let's shadow him."

T.J. reached into his bag and pulled out a

bright red scarf. Two or three gumballs fell out and rolled across the sidewalk.

As T.J. draped the scarf over his head and started to tie it under his chin, Dottie said, "Hey, that's mine!"

"That's okay," T.J. assured her. "I don't mind." He reached into his bag again, pulled out a long string of blue and green beads, and put it around his neck.

"And my necklace," Dottie added. "I didn't say you could borrow my things. What are you supposed to be?"

"Shhh!" T.J. said. "I'm in disguise. Okay, let's go."

Jay looked at T.J.'s costume and rolled his eyes, but all he said was, "I don't think we should all follow that guy at once. We might be a little, um—"

"Conspicuous," Dottie suggested.

"Crazy-looking," said Laurie.

"Crowded," T.J. added. "Besides, the guy already knows Laurie. He'd catch on to her in a minute. But he'll never suspect me. Come on, Jay, he's getting away from us."

"Hey, what about—" Dottie began. But her two brothers were already crossing the street. She turned to Laurie. "*Boys!*" she said scornfully.

Laurie smiled. "I think they're kind of cute," she replied. "Weird, but cute."

The guard at the front door of Glover's Department Store frowned as Jay and T.J. came in, but they paid no attention. They couldn't expect him to know that they were famous detectives—well, detectives who were going to be famous.

The guy in the two-tone jacket was not near the door. They walked over two aisles and stopped near a display of perfume.

"Do you see him anywhere?" T.J. asked in an undertone. He pretended to be interested in the array of perfume sprayers on the counter.

"Nope," Jay replied. He checked his camera to be sure that he had enough shots left. "Maybe he went to a different floor."

T.J. picked up one of the sprayers and studied the label. "Deadly Passion," he read. "I wonder what it smells like."

"Can I help you, young lady?" a voice said from right in back of him.

T.J. jumped in surprise, and his hand squeezed the bulb of the perfume sprayer. Jay turned just in time to get a cloud of Deadly Passion right in the face. He started to cough and choke.

The salesperson gave T.J. a hard look. "That isn't something to play with, you know," she pointed out. "That is a very expensive French perfume."

"It's a pretty smelly one, too," Jay said, rubbing at his face.

"Sorry, ma'am," said T.J. "It was an accident."

Something about his voice made her look at him more closely. She opened her mouth to say something, but Jay grabbed T.J.'s arm and pulled him away.

"Sorry, ma'am," he said. "We've got to run."

"I don't think your disguise fooled her," Jay told T.J. as soon as they were out of the salesperson's hearing.

"Really? Hold on a minute." He took off the scarf and necklace and stuffed them into his school bag, then began to rummage around. "How about a beard?" he said. "I like wearing beards."

"Later for that," Jay said urgently. "There's our guy now!"

At the far end of the aisle, a maroon and yellow jacket was just disappearing.

"Come on," Jay exclaimed. "I want to get close enough to get a shot of him."

T.J. paused just long enough to put on a big floppy green cap and pull it down over his forehead. Then he hurried after Jay.

The two boys stopped at the end of the aisle and looked around, puzzled. The teen-ager was nowhere in sight. Where had he gone?

T.J. pointed to a half-open door almost hidden between two cabinets. "Maybe he went through there," he suggested.

Jay wrinkled his forehead. "I don't know," he said "It says 'Employees Only.'"

T.J. pulled his cap lower over his ears and said, "Yeah, but if he's an international jewel thief, maybe he doesn't always obey signs. Let's take a look."

The door led into a short, dark hallway. Cardboard cartons were stacked almost to the ceiling on either side. T.J. looked at them nervously and said, "On second thought, I don't think he came this way, after all. Let's go back."

"No, there's a door up ahead," Jay replied. "Come on, let's see if it's unlocked."

He pushed it open, and they stepped out onto a small loading dock overlooking the alley behind the store. On one side, a small metal dumpster on wheels took up most of the room. In the other direction, a narrow ramp led down to the level of the pavement.

"Nothing here," Jay observed. "We ought to—"

"What was that?" T.J. demanded. "It sounded like a car door."

"I think it was from just around the corner," Jay replied. He started down the narrow ramp. T.J. was close behind him. Suddenly there was a screech of metal, followed by a low, ominous rumbling sound.

The two boys whirled around. The metal dumpster was rolling down the ramp, right toward them. It was gathering speed. And there was no room to escape!

C·H·A·P·T·E·R
4

*T*he heavy metal dumpster was bearing down on them, rolling faster and faster down the narrow ramp. Jay glanced frantically over his shoulder. The end of the ramp was too far away for them to run, and there was no room to scrape by between the dumpster and the side of the building.

"Jump, T.J.," he shouted. "Jump!"

He grabbed the pipe railing and vaulted over it. T.J. was right behind him. A moment later they were both sprawled on the muddy stone pavement. And a moment after that, the dumpster rumbled off the end of the ramp and crashed into a brick wall.

"That could have been us it hit," T.J. said. "Oo-wee, that was close!"

"Hey," someone shouted. They looked up.

A young man in shirt-sleeves was standing in the doorway.

"What do you kids think you're doing?" he demanded. "Don't you know you're not allowed back here? Look what you did to our dumpster!"

"Look what it almost did to us," Jay said. "We didn't touch it, but it nearly ran over us."

A worried look passed over the man's face. "It must have been an accident," he said. "Maybe the foot brake slipped. Anyway, you're not supposed to be back here."

"What about a guy in a maroon and yellow jacket that says 'JUNIOR' on it?" T.J. replied. "Is he supposed to be back here?"

"I don't know what you're talking about," the man said, but he sounded as if he did.

"Come on, T.J.," said Jay. "Let's get back to the others."

At that moment, an engine started with a roar. A white van pulled out of a parking space just beyond the loading dock, only a few feet from where the dumpster had been sitting. It sped toward the street. Jay and T.J. ran after it, but by the time they reached the sidewalk, it was half a block away.

"Could you see who was in it?" Jay demanded.

"Too far," T.J. replied, panting. "You?"

Jay shook his head. "I didn't even get a photo of the license plate. We'd better warn the others to keep an eye out for that van. Something tells me it's an important clue."

That evening Phil Klink cooked his famous lasagna. He didn't exactly cook it, since it was already waiting in the freezer, and it wasn't exactly his, since Patty had made it in the first place. But it *was* famous, at least among his five foster kids. And as he pointed out, he *was* the one who took it out of the freezer, heated it in the oven, and brought it to the table. That had to count for something.

As they were finishing their lasagna, Jimmy said, "Chief? Do you know if there are any gangs of jewel thieves in town?"

T.J. swallowed a mouthful of milk the wrong way. He coughed loudly, spraying milk onto the table. Jay mopped it up while Lee pounded T.J. on the back.

Once things calmed down, Phil said, "What was that you asked about, Jimmy? Jewel thieves?"

"Um-hum," Jimmy replied. "See, Cosmic Cop is after an intergalactic jewel thief named Hot Rocks, and I was wondering . . ."

The Chief laughed. "You kids should know all about that. Especially since you helped capture that jewel thief at Shockly Manor."

He wiped a bit of tomato sauce from his beard. "No, there hasn't been much going on in the way of jewel thefts. Now, pickpockets—that's another story. Everybody in town has pockets, and a lot of the pockets have something of value in them."

Jay felt in his pocket. The little wad of tissue that contained Laurie's diamond was still there. What if someone stole it from him? He was starting to wish he hadn't agreed to hang onto the gem for her.

"Have the police caught the pickpocket yet?" asked Dottie.

Phil shook his head. "Nope, and they're none too happy about it, either. He struck again this afternoon, at Glover's. I guess their clerks were too busy watching for shoplifters to notice a pickpocket."

T.J. opened his mouth to say that they had been at Glover's themselves that afternoon, but somebody kicked him under the table. "Hey," he exclaimed, "what's the idea?"

Jimmy, Lee, and Dottie looked puzzled. Jay looked angelic. "You just wait," T.J. growled. "I'll get you for that."

"No arguing at the table, please," Mrs. Klink said. "Are all of you ready for dessert?"

After clearing the table and washing the dishes, the kids raced out to their clubhouse. It was time to start making some serious plans.

"The whole case centers around Toots' Sweets," Jimmy declared. "I say we go back and question Miss Kossmeyer again."

Dottie was curled up in a pile of pillows. "We didn't get much out of her this afternoon," she pointed out.

"This time *I'll* handle it," Jimmy said. "I'll fix her with my steely blue eyes—"

"They're still brown, the same as always," said Jay.

"Whatever," Jimmy replied. "I'll grill her until she breaks down and tells everything she knows."

"But what if she doesn't know anything?" Lee demanded. "Maybe the gang only used the gumball machine at her store that one time. Maybe they've switched to another gumball machine by now."

"Good point, Lee," Jay said. "It sounds to me as if we have to check out every gumball machine in town. There's something mysterious going on, and that's the only way we're going to get to the bottom of it."

"That's a lot of gumball machines," Dottie said.

Lee grinned and said, "Yeah!" He rubbed his stomach.

Jimmy pulled out his pad and started making a list. The others chipped in names and locations. Finally Jimmy sat back and whistled. "That's more than a dozen places," he announced. "We're going to have to split up into teams."

"I want to work alone this time," T.J. announced. "And we should all use our code names."

Jay shrugged. "Okay with me, I guess," he replied. "Lee, why don't you and Jimmy team up—"

"Smudge and Jaws," T.J. insisted.

"Right," said Jay. "Smudge and Jaws. Dottie —I mean, Short Stuff—can go with me."

"Good thinking, Clicker," T.J. said.

Jay rolled his eyes at T.J. "Thanks a bunch, Smoke Screen," he replied. "Now, if that's settled, let's divide up that list of candy shops . . ."

The next morning, after breakfast, Jay and Dottie rode downtown and parked their bikes in the rack in front of the Leaning Tower of Pizza. Their first objective, Dandy Candy, was just down the block, on the other side of the Coffee Stop. A moment later, a police car pulled up in front of the cafe. The two officers hurried inside.

"Time for a coffee break," Jay said.

Dottie frowned. "I wonder," she replied. "They looked awfully serious."

They stopped by the door and peered inside. The cops were standing near the front. Their notebooks were open, and they were talking to a woman who kept pointing to her open purse, then waving her hands around.

Jay looked at Dottie. "What do you think, Short Stuff?" he asked.

"The same as you, Clicker," she answered. "The town pickpocket strikes again. We ought to go after that guy."

Jay laughed. "One case at a time! Still. . . ." He snapped a picture of the woman and the two officers. When the flash went off, all three turned and looked. Jay smiled and waved. They didn't wave back.

"Come on," he muttered to Dottie. "Let's leave before they have time to decide if they're mad at me."

The kids went into Dandy Candy and glanced around. Dottie nudged Jay and pointed to the rack of gumball machines just to the left of the door.

"Three of them," she said softly. "And look, the one in the middle has an 'Out of Order' sign on it."

"Just like at Toots' Sweets," Jay replied. "Let's see if we can get answers to a few questions."

The owner smiled at them from behind the cash register. "You kids need anything?" he asked.

"Um, we were looking at the gumball machines," Jay began.

The smile disappeared. "What about them?" the man demanded.

"Why isn't the middle one working?" Dottie asked. "I like the prizes better in that one."

"You'll have to ask Bonomo that," he replied. "It has nothing to do with me."

"Bonomo? Who's that?" Jay quickly asked.

"The company that put them in. Bonomo Novelties, over in the warehouse district." The owner studied their faces for a moment. "Hey, what's so interesting about those gumball machines? You wouldn't be—"

"Nothing," Jay said.

"We were just asking," Dottie added. She smiled at the candy store owner.

"Oh, sure," the man said.

Jay suddenly elbowed her and muttered, "Duck!"

"What?" She glanced around. The teenager in the maroon and yellow jacket was crossing the sidewalk. He was heading straight for the candy store.

Dottie and Jay hurried to the back of the store and watched from behind a rack of paperback books. Junior came in, nodded to the owner, and took a big ring of keys from his pocket.

"Look, he's opening the gumball machines," Dottie whispered. "What's he doing?"

"Refilling them, I think," Jay whispered back. After a moment, he added, "He's taking the money out and closing the machines. Come on, let's follow him."

They raced out of the store just in time to see Junior climb behind the wheel of a white van. On the door was painted, "Bonomo Novelties."

"Look!" Dottie exclaimed. "In the front seat—it's that fat man!"

"You know what else," Jay said grimly. "I've seen that van before. It was in the alley behind Glover's yesterday. It drove off right after T.J. and I were almost flattened! I bet that Bonomo Novelties is fencing stolen jewels!"

C·H·A·P·T·E·R
5

*J*ay and Dottie leaped on their bikes.

"I can't wait to tell the others about this," said Jay.

"Yeah," Dottie said. "Now we know that Junior works for the people who fill the gumball machines."

"And he's real friendly with that fat man."

"Which means what?" Dottie suddenly asked.

"Don't ask me," Jay exclaimed. "That's why we have a team of experts." Jay thought about what he had just said. "Well," he said slowly. "At least we have a *team*."

"That's right," said Dottie. "Now all we have to do is find them."

"Let's get moving," Jimmy said. "We've still got two more places on our list." Jimmy and Lee were checking out their fifth candy store.

"Just a second," Lee replied. "Is the owner still watching us?"

Jimmy glanced over his shoulder. "Like a hawk," he said. "Why?"

Lee sighed. "I wanted to try to lift some prints off the gumball machine in the middle," he explained. "The one with the 'Out of Order' sign on it. Doesn't it look newer than the other two? Why should it be out of order?"

"Beats me." Jimmy looked around as the front door opened. "Look," he said, "it's Junior and that fat man. Don't let them see us!"

Jimmy and Lee hurried to the far side of the store and began studying a display of hand-dipped chocolate candy in a large glass case. Nobody would have guessed that the glass was acting as a mirror, and that they could see everything that happened behind them.

Junior went straight to the gumball machines and started doing something to them. Meanwhile, the fat man stood at the counter. He and the owner talked in very low voices. Jimmy strained his ears, but he couldn't make out a word.

Junior straightened up and went over to the

counter. "I'm done here," he said. "You ready?"

The fat man took an envelope from his inside coat pocket and handed it to the candy store owner. "You're a wise man, Mr. Dash," he said. "I like a man who can see his own best interests."

As the fat man and Junior turned to leave, Jimmy said, "Let's get to our bikes. We've got to follow those guys!"

The two men stood talking on the sidewalk for a moment, then Junior climbed into the white van. The fat man turned and walked away.

"You follow the van," Jimmy said quickly. "I'll take the fat man."

"Right, Jaws," Lee said. He jumped onto his bike and pedaled furiously down the street.

Jimmy rode more slowly, keeping half a block behind his target. When the fat man reached Green Street, he turned left and stopped outside a store that advertised, "Italian Pastry—Ice Cream Specialties." He looked at the window for a while, then went inside.

Jimmy parked his bike and waited a couple of minutes before following the man in. The waitress was just putting an enormous banana split on the table in front of him.

"Thank you, young lady," the man said. "Tell me, is the owner here this morning?"

"Sure," the waitress said. "He's out back. I'll get him."

The man who came out from the back room was wearing a white apron and a baker's cap. Jimmy noticed a smudge of flour on his cheek.

"Ah," the fat man said. "Mr. Falcone, I presume?"

The baker shook his head. "That's my partner," he said. "I'm Carlo Maltese. What can I do for you?"

"My name is Blackbird, sir. I'm a stranger in Dozerville, but I have already heard very good things about your pastries. You do special orders, don't you?"

"You bet," Maltese said. "You tell me what you want, I make it for you."

Blackbird rubbed his hands together. "Excellent," he exclaimed. "Excellent! I can tell that you're a man who enjoys his profession. I like a man who enjoys his profession. You'll be hearing from me, Mr. Maltese."

"Anytime before eight," the baker said. "You better eat your banana split, Mister. The ice cream's melting."

Maltese returned to the back room. Blackbird ate a few spoonfuls of his ice cream, then looked up and met Jimmy's glance.

"Well, young man," he said. "Please join me at my table. Aren't you going to order one of these magnificent concoctions?"

Jimmy remembered all the warnings he had heard about talking to strangers. Surely they didn't apply to detectives on active duty, though. He sat down across from Mr. Blackbird and said, "I'm not hungry, Mister. I had a lot of gumballs this morning."

He watched carefully to see how the fat man reacted to this. But the man just smiled strangely and took another bite of his banana split.

"I like gumballs," Jimmy continued. He was feeling very daring. "I like to get them out of gumball machines. It's a funny thing, though. A whole bunch of the gumball machines in town seem to be broken. Why do you think that is?"

"Sheer bad luck, I suppose," Blackbird replied. "Are you sure you will not accept a Chocolate Mountain? Or perhaps a Fudge-Nut Delight? My treat, of course."

Jimmy felt his stomach rumble, but he told it to behave itself. "No, thank you," he said. "I'm not really that interested in ice cream. What I really like is diamonds—big diamonds."

"Indeed, sir?" retorted Blackbird with that strange smile. "A very pleasant failing. But since I am not offering you any big diamonds, will you accept a strawberry frappé instead? I hate to see a man go hungry."

Jimmy swallowed hard. It had been a long

time since breakfast, and Mr. Blackbird's banana split looked really yummy. He was about to say yes, when he remembered why he was there. He straightened up, looked the fat man straight in the eye, and said, "Keep it, Mr. Blackbird. Before long, you may need all the strawberry frappés you can get."

Blackbird nodded. "Very well, sir," he said. "I respect your decision. But I suggest you keep your curiosity about diamonds and gumball machines and other matters that don't concern you under control—under *strict* control—at least until after tomorrow."

Jimmy leaned back in his chair and narrowed his eyes. "Yeah?" he replied. "We'll see about that."

The fat man leaned forward. The front of his shirt almost scraped what was left of the whipped cream off the top of his banana split. He too narrowed his eyes as he said, "So we shall, young man, so we shall. But let me give you a friendly warning."

He waved a chubby finger in front of Jimmy's face. Jimmy leaned back farther.

"Your questions," Blackbird said in a hard voice, "are indiscreet. It is not very wise to keep asking such questions. They could cost me, and my, ah, my associates, a great deal of trouble and money. And believe me, young man, my associates wouldn't like that. They wouldn't like that at *all*."

On the word "all," he thrust his forefinger right at Jimmy's face. Jimmy ducked back and felt his chair start to tip over backwards. An instant later he was sprawled out on the floor of the ice cream parlor. His elbows and shoulders, which had broken the force of the fall, hurt a lot. But he paid no attention to them. He was too busy thinking about the amazing thing that had just happened.

Now he knew he was a real detective, working on a real case. He'd put pressure on the bad guy, and the fat man had cracked like that nursery rhyme egg.

Mr. Blackbird had just offered him a bribe to give up his investigation. And when he didn't go along, the fat man had threatened ... No. More like he said ... Well, actually he had *hinted*, that Jimmy had just made a number of deadly enemies.

C·H·A·P·T·E·R
6

*T*he sidewalk artist ambled along Elm Street, glancing at the sky, the stores, and the passing cars and pedestrians as he went. A lot of the people he passed glanced at him, too, then smiled.

He *did* look a little odd for that part of town. He was very short, and his old suit jacket was very long, with the sleeves rolled halfway to the elbow. His black hair was very long, too. And his bushy, long, bright red moustache covered the lower half of his face.

The artist stopped in front of Glover's Department Store to shift his ragged portfolio to his other hand. The guard inside the front door stared at him. He looked as if he was trying to remember something. The artist gave him a cheery wave and walked on.

Just down the block, across the street from

Toots' Sweets, he stopped and looked around. Then he put down his portfolio, took out a handful of drawings, and started taping them to the side of the building.

Once he was done, he stood back and studied the effect. There were drawings of houses and spaceships and trees, of horses and cars and forts, and even some of people. A few were done in markers, but most were in crayon.

He nodded to himself. It looked like a very professional display. He sat down on the sidewalk next to the building, took out a box of crayons and a pad of paper, and started to sketch Toots' Sweets.

A few minutes passed. Suddenly a voice said, "T.J., imagine finding you here. Are you selling your drawings? Why are you dressed so funny? And why have you got that on your face? It looks like a fuzzy red caterpillar!"

T.J. looked up. Laurie Peters was standing there, blocking his view of Toots' Sweets. She was wearing bright red jeans, a red and yellow shirt, and matching high-tops.

"Mommy," she said, turning to a woman in a sort of gypsy skirt and top. "This is T.J. He's in my class. Isn't it exciting? He's become an artist."

"Uh, Laurie," T.J. began, "could you not let on that you know me?"

"Not know you?" she said loudly. "Why not? Of course I know you, T.J., even with all that extra hair and that silly moustache. What's it for, anyway?"

He spoke softly, through clenched teeth. "I'm undercover," he said. "I'm working on . . . you know what. Now will you please go away?"

"Undercover," Laurie shrieked. "You mean . . ." She looked around, wide-eyed. "You must be watching that gumball machine," she continued. "How exciting!"

T.J. took a deep breath. "Look," he said quietly. "I don't want you to blow my cover. If you won't go away, at least pretend you're looking at the drawings."

"Laurie," Mrs. Peters said, "we have a lot more shopping to do. You'll see your friend at school next week."

"Okay, Mommy," Laurie replied. "Bye-bye, T.J. I hope your art show goes well."

As they walked away, T.J. heard Mrs. Peters say, "Your friend seems nice, Laurie, but he certainly is a little strange. Does he always wear a fake moustache?"

T.J. shook his head. Some people just didn't understand detective work. He settled down again, to wait and watch.

Five minutes passed. It was warm in the sun, and he was starting to feel drowsy. He yawned

and felt his eyelids start to droop. Maybe he was wasting his time watching Toots' Sweets. Sure, Laurie had found that diamond there the day before, but what were the odds that there were any more? The chances were . . .

A car door slammed. T.J. opened his eyes and sat up straight. Had he fallen asleep? He looked around. A dark sedan had pulled up across the street, in front of the candy store. The trunk lid was up, and three men in jeans and sweat shirts were taking big, oddly-shaped cases out and stacking them on the sidewalk. One of them slammed the trunk closed, and they all picked up the cases and carried them inside Toots' Sweets.

T.J. couldn't imagine what the cases held, but he was sure of one thing. It wasn't gumballs or peppermint sticks.

Something was going on inside the candy store, that was obvious. And it was his duty to find out what it was. He took his drawings down from the wall and packed them in the portfolio, then crossed the street and peeked in the window of Toots' Sweets.

At first the store looked empty. Then he saw Miss Kossmeyer. She was standing near the doorway to the storeroom. It looked as if she was talking to somebody in back. The men who had carried the cases inside?

"Okay, Smoke Screen," T.J. muttered to himself. "This is your chance to show your stuff. Get in there and find out what's going on."

He walked over to the door, as casually as he could, and glanced inside. Miss Kossmeyer was still facing the other way. Holding his breath, he eased the door open, just wide enough to slip in. He was halfway through when something grabbed him. He looked down. The pocket of his big suit jacket was caught on the door handle. He backed up and tried to unsnag it.

"I can't help being nervous," Miss Kossmeyer said.

T.J. looked around frantically. The candy store owner still had her back to him, but over her shoulder he could see one of the men from the car. At any moment the man would see him, too. He tugged at his jacket and heard a ripping sound. He was free. He was also missing a pocket.

He ducked behind a set of shelves full of jars of penny candies. By moving two of the jars, he could see through the shelf without being seen.

"Don't worry," one of the men told Miss Kossmeyer. "We know what we're doing."

"Oh, I'm sure you do," she replied. "It's just that I've never been mixed up in something like this. Something so . . . I don't know."

"Don't worry," the man repeated. "Everything's set for noon tomorrow. It'll be over before you know it. Who knows? You might even enjoy the excitement."

Miss Kossmeyer brushed her hair back from her face. "I hope so," she said. "If only I don't have to answer a lot of questions. I was never very good at keeping secrets."

The man frowned. "Well, you'd better practice," he said in a gruff voice. "If any of this gets out, some people could find themselves in a lot of trouble."

"I know, I know," Miss Kossmeyer said. "I did promise to keep quiet when I agreed to let your organization use my store. I still can't believe how much money I'll be getting."

The man laughed. "In our business, there's usually plenty of money to spread around," he explained. "We'd better get going. We've got some other arrangements to take care of.

"Mike, Charlie," he called. "Aren't you done yet?"

One of the other men appeared in the door to the storeroom. "All set, Jerry," he said.

He glanced around the store. His gaze met T.J.'s. T.J. ducked, but not soon enough.

"Hey," the man shouted. "There's someone over there spying on us!"

T.J. made a dash in the direction of the door, but the one called Jerry was blocking it.

"What are you doing here, kid?" he demanded. "What did you overhear?"

T.J. glanced over his shoulder. The man who had spotted him was hurrying toward him. He looked very big and very mad.

T.J. straightened up and said, in the most innocent voice he could manage, "Me, Mister? I wasn't doing anything. I was just looking at the lemon drops."

The man gave a harsh laugh. "Yeah? We'll see about that."

Trapped! thought T.J. Trapped by crooks, in a candy store. What a way to go!

C·H·A·P·T·E·R
7

*T*he man in back of T.J. put his hand on the boy's shoulder. "We don't like nosy people prying into our business," he growled.

From the back of the candy shop, Tootsie Kossmeyer cried, "What are you doing? Let him go!"

"We will," Jerry said. "Just as soon as he tells us what he was doing here." He started toward T.J.

T.J. saw his chance to escape. The minute Jerry moved away from the door, T.J. wriggled loose from the other man's grip and ducked under a table that held a display of old-fashioned candies. The two men started after him, but they had to go around the table. That slowed them down.

As he ran past the candy display, T.J.

scooped up a handful of hard peppermint balls. Near the door he scattered them on the floor. It seemed a shame to waste good candy, but this was an emergency.

He was reaching for the door handle when Jerry came running up. His friend was right behind him.

"Hey, wait a minute," the man shouted. But at that moment his foot landed on a peppermint ball and shot out from under him. He fell backward, and knocked his partner down too.

T.J. bolted out the door and took a quick, panicky look up and down the street. Behind him, Jerry and the other guy were still yelling for him to stop. They would be back on their feet any minute now. He could try to run, but their car was sitting right in front of the store. How could he even hope to get away from them?

His eyes suddenly lit up. There, just a little way down the block on the other side of the street, was a familiar wood-bodied station wagon. And at the same moment he spotted it, he saw Phil Klink coming out of the True-to-Type stationery store.

As the front door of Toots' Sweets crashed open behind him, T.J. dashed across the street and jumped into the front seat of the station wagon. His foster father had just gotten behind the wheel.

———•———

"What—?" he said.

T.J. pulled off the black wig and the bushy red moustache. "Hi, Chief," he said breathlessly. "It's me, T.J. Going my way?"

Phil chuckled and shook his head. "Honestly, son," he said. "Where did you get that lip fuzz?"

"I made it myself," T.J. replied proudly. "I bet it fooled you, didn't it?"

"Well, it was certainly, uh, different," the Chief admitted. He signaled a left turn and pulled out into traffic. "Black hair and a red moustache is an unusual combination."

T.J. grinned. "I know, that's the idea," he explained. "See, everybody will pay attention to that, so they won't notice *me*. Neat, huh?"

Phil nodded. "That's clever thinking, T.J.," he said. "But I worry that these disguises are getting a little out of hand. There's nothing wrong with the way you look when you're not wearing one, you know."

"I know that," T.J. replied. "But if we're going to solve mysteries and catch crooks, we've got to be crafty, right? If they don't know who I am, they won't know that they have to be careful around me. It's like I'm almost invisible."

Phil chuckled again. "Okay, okay," he said. "I know when I'm outnumbered. I won't say any more about it just now. But take my advice and get rid of that red moustache. It's a little too old for you."

"Whatever you say, Chief," T.J. said. He was about to add that the bad guys already had seen the moustache, anyway. Then he remembered that the Clues Kids hadn't yet told Phil about their new case. "Er," he added, quickly changing the subject, "what brought you to town this morning?"

"A few errands, that's all," Phil replied. "And I found time to have a cup of coffee with a couple of old friends who are still on the force. I bet they'd like to have the power to be invisible just now."

T.J. looked over at him. "What do you mean?" he asked.

"You remember that pickpocket we were talking about? He's been really busy the last couple of days." The Chief paused and shook his head in puzzlement. "He moves around a lot, too," he continued. "People have had their pockets picked in half a dozen different places all over town—Glover's and the Coffee Stop, and even a hardware store clear over on Green Street."

T.J. blinked in surprise. Something about the list of places sounded familiar to him, but he couldn't think what. He was about to say so to Phil, then he changed his mind and

kept his mouth shut. He could always open it when he had something a little more definite to say.

Lee swooped down the block, pedaling as fast as he could. His legs ached, and a stitch burned in his side, but he didn't mind. He felt very proud of himself. He had never ridden better or faster. He had managed to keep the white van in sight block after block, turn after turn, all the way from the middle of town out here to the warehouse district.

Up ahead, the van turned right onto a narrow side street. Lee tucked his head down and leaned over the handlebars to gain a little more speed. It seemed to take forever, but at last he sped around the corner and—

His mouth fell open. He let the bike drift to a stop. The street, lined with tall, brick warehouses, was empty. The van had vanished. There hadn't been enough time for it to reach the other end and turn off, but it was nowhere in sight.

A superstitious shiver rippled down Lee's back. Was the van *real*? Then he shrugged and laughed at himself. Had Sherlock Holmes been scared when he faced the fearsome Hound of the Baskervilles? Of course not! And a white van was a lot less scary than an enormous dog with big teeth and bad breath!

He rode slowly up the block, studying the old buildings on either side. Some of them had loading bays set into them. A few were even built around small courtyards. Many of the windows were boarded or bricked up. They made the area feel like a ghost town.

Lee shivered again, then almost fell over when a cat yowled and darted across the street in front of him. As he swerved, a sign on the warehouse to his left caught his eye. BONOMO NOVELTIES, it said. That was the name on the van!

An arched passageway, dark and gloomy as a tunnel, led through the front part of the building to a stone-paved courtyard. Lee leaned his bike against the wall, walked through the passage, and peeked carefully around the corner.

He had to bite his lip to keep from letting out a shout of triumph. The white van was in the courtyard, parked next to a raised loading platform. There wasn't anybody in sight.

He tiptoed over to the van and tried the doors. Locked. He tried to peer inside, but he couldn't see a thing. He was about to retreat to the street when he saw something wonderful. Someone had closed the rear door by pushing on the window with his right hand. And he had left a reminder behind—the clearest set of fingerprints Lee had ever seen!

He quickly pulled his belt pouch around to the front and unzipped it. The tin of powder was there, and a little tube for blowing it over the prints, and special sticky paper to lift them. One of these days he planned to get a camera with a closeup lens, but he knew how to make do with what he had.

At last the careful, delicate job was done. He rolled up the paper and tucked it in his pouch, then turned to go. But when he turned, he bumped his nose into a maroon and yellow jacket with "JUNIOR" written across the front. Bumping into the jacket would have been okay with Lee. Unfortunately, someone was in it.

Lee looked up at the face of a very angry teenager. "Okay, you little brat. I've got you this time. You're going to tell me everything. And I'd better like what I hear—if you want to stay healthy."

C·H·A·P·T·E·R
8

*L*ee glanced around quickly, but he couldn't see any way to escape. In fact, he couldn't see much of anything at all, except that maroon and yellow jacket.

"Who, me?" he began. He tried giving Junior a combination of wide eyes and an innocent smile. The teenager did not seem impressed.

"I don't know what you mean," Lee continued. If he was being scored on originality, he had already lost.

"Don't give me that," Junior retorted. He shook his fist under Lee's nose. It was a very large, bumpy-looking fist, and there were rough, bumpy-looking rings on two of the fingers. Getting in the way of that fist ranked pretty low on Lee's list of fun things to do.

"You and your friends have been on my case for a couple of days now," Junior said. "You think I didn't notice the way you've been following me? You think I like a bunch of little brats spying on me? Well, I got news for you. I don't."

"Really, Mister," Lee replied, letting a quaver into his voice, "I was just riding by on my bike, and I saw this courtyard, and I thought it looked interesting, like a place you'd see on a TV show or something. So I came back to look around, and . . . and that's all."

Junior sneered. "Sure you did. But I saw you at my last stop. You were inside the candy store with your pal, and you followed me outside and got on your bike. And don't try to tell me it wasn't you. Not unless you have a twin brother."

Lee opened his mouth to say that he had *two* twin brothers, or at least two brothers who were twins. But he stopped himself. He couldn't think of a way to say it that didn't make him sound like a wise guy.

"I'll tell you what really happened," the teenager continued. "You followed me here on your bike. You saw the van parked here, and you saw I wasn't around. So you decided to break into the van and steal whatever you could. You were monkeying with the lock on the rear door when I caught you."

"I was not!" Lee declared.

"Sure you were. I saw you. You must have thought you could get away with a year's supply of gumballs, right?" Junior snickered. "Heh, heh. Not from me, you don't, you little thief."

Lee clenched his fists. He could feel his face turning red with anger. "I am *not* a thief," he shouted. "You're the one who's a thief, not me!"

Junior grabbed Lee's collar and started to shake him, but Lee was not going to be silenced. "We're on to you and your friends," he exclaimed. "We know you're a gang of big-time jewel thieves. That doesn't worry us a bit. We're going to stop your fiendish plan and put you away for a long time!"

The last sentence was a quotation from a recent episode of *Cosmic Cop*. Lee expected it to have a big effect on Junior. It did, but not exactly the effect he expected.

The teenager suddenly let go of Lee's jacket and started to laugh. "Jewel thieves!" he repeated. "Boy, wait 'til Mr. Blackbird hears this one. He'll die!"

Junior shook his head. "Listen, kid," he said, "you don't know how far off base you really are. So why don't you just get out of here and stop bugging me, okay?"

He turned and walked away, still laughing.

Lee watched him for a moment, unsure what to do next. Then he retrieved his bike and rode toward home.

But he felt confused. Junior's reaction had been weird. Like he really wasn't a crook. *Maybe he's bluffing*, Lee thought. But if he wasn't a jewel thief, what *was* he up to? And if he was a thief—

Lee was getting a headache from all the confusing possibilities. And finally, all he could think about was getting home—where he could put his feet up, and relax.

"Here's another paw print on the side of the refrigerator," Dottie announced.

"That cat," Lee grumbled. "Why couldn't he stay in one place?"

Jimmy looked up from his notebook. "Maybe Prowler didn't like having his paw dipped in ink," he suggested.

"Or being held still while you took his print," Jay added.

Lee turned from putting away the mop. "Okay, okay," he said. "I told him I was sorry, didn't I? He didn't have to run all the way across the kitchen and jump up on top of the fridge. How am I going to get up there to clean it off?"

T.J. grinned. "Try taking a running jump," he said. "That's the way Prowler did it."

"Wise guy," Lee retorted as he took the stepstool out of the broom closet and set it up next to the refrigerator.

Jimmy laughed at the argument between his brothers. "You wouldn't think a little cat could cause so much trouble."

"Don't forget how we got Prowler in the first place," said T.J. "You saw him when we were on that Shockly Manor case."

"Yeah," Lee taunted. "You said it would be neat to have a cat. So you brought him home—"

"Hidden under your jacket," Dottie added.

"All right, all right," Jimmy grumbled. "So I fell for a cute little kitten—and now he's gotten bigger. So sue me!"

"Don't give me any ideas," Lee replied.

At that moment, Jay decided it was time to take charge. "Okay, guys," he said. "We've collected a lot of clues. But what do they add up to? And what do we do next?"

"You know," T.J. began, "there's something funny about the way we keep crossing paths with that pickpocket, but we never run into him."

Dottie nodded vigorously. "That's right. It's like he's always someplace a few minutes ahead of us or behind us. It's weird."

Jay shrugged. "We've been all over downtown since we started this case," he pointed out. "It figures that a pickpocket would hang out where there are lots of pockets to pick. Anyway, I think we should finish one case before we start another one."

"Something big is going to happen tomorrow," said Jimmy. "That fat man told me to stop asking questions for one more day. At least, I think that's what he said." He laughed. "It was right about then that my chair tipped over backwards."

"It all fits," T.J. declared. "Remember what that guy told Miss Kossmeyer? He said it was all set for noon tomorrow. That must be when the big caper comes off. And it's up to us to foil it."

"I don't understand," said Dottie. "*What* big caper? What are they going to do at Toots' Sweets that's so important?"

"We don't really know," Jay admitted, making a cross face. "But at least we know *when* and *where*. Tomorrow we'll find out *what*. Now here's what I think we should do . . ."

It was an ordinary Saturday morning in downtown Dozerville. The sun was shining, the breeze was blowing, and the birds were nestled in the trees.

A few yards down the block from the Toots' Sweets candy store, three boys were hunkered down on the sidewalk, playing marbles. The right season for marbles was long past, but maybe no one had told them. Or maybe they simply liked marbles.

A few yards up the block from the candy store, a short, bearded street peddler was selling old magazines and children's books. Not that anyone was buying any. Mrs. Costanza wanted a back issue of *Travel Italy*, but when she heard that the price was ten dollars, she shrugged, drew a little circle around her ear with her index finger, and walked away.

A few minutes before noon, the peddler strolled down the block and stopped to watch the marble players. "See that big truck parked in front of Toots' Sweets?" he said softly. His voice sounded exactly like T.J.'s. "A few minutes ago those three guys I tangled with yesterday climbed into the back of it."

"And that's not all," said Jimmy. "Look, Blackbird's getting into the back, too!"

Jay snorted. "All we need now is Junior," he said. "Why isn't he here?"

"Hey," Lee said excitedly. "That lady's about to put her money in the middle gumball machine. Look, the 'Out of Order' sign is gone."

Out of the corner of his eye, Jay saw the Chief's ancient station wagon arrive at the curb. At that moment, the woman in front of the candy shop reached into the gumball ma-

chine and pulled out a long, gleaming pearl
necklace.

"Let's go," Jay said urgently. "Don't let her
escape!"

The boys sprang up and dashed toward the
store, just as Dottie and the Chief climbed out
of the car. T.J. and Lee took the lead, with Jay
right on their heels. Jimmy lagged a little
behind. Something was bothering him—something he had seen without noticing it. But
what?

He glanced in the direction of the parked
truck and gasped. Attached to the side of the
truck was a small metal flap. It had been shut
before, but now it was wide open. Something
round and black was sticking out of it, something that looked a lot like the muzzle of a
machine gun. And it was aimed straight at
the Chief!

C·H·A·P·T·E·R
9

"*L*ook out!" Jimmy yelled.

Jay, Lee, and T.J. looked around, saw what was happening, and jumped into action. Lee and T.J. ran forward like football tackles, right for the woman with the pearl necklace. She let out a shriek. Then she and the two boys crashed into Mr. Appleton's fruit stand. There were mashed bananas everywhere.

Jay rushed over to the Chief. "Back!" he shouted, and gave him a shove. From the other side, Dottie tugged at their foster father's coat, trying to drag him out of the line of fire.

"Now hold on," Phil began. "What do you two think you're—" But Dottie and Jay just kept pushing and tugging. Explanations would have to wait.

●

From his position next to the truck, Jimmy watched what was happening as he made a move of his own. The bad guys could always change their aim, or even pick a new target . . . but only if they could see to aim.

He bent over to stay out of sight, and ran alongside the truck. Grabbing the metal flap with both hands, he slammed it shut. Someone inside the truck started shouting angrily.

Jimmy caught his twin brother's eye, grinned, and gave him a V sign for victory. The Clues Kids had triumphed again.

A crowd was starting to gather, drawn by the commotion.

"Dottie," Phil Klink said calmly, "would you please let go of my coat? Thanks. Now, Jay," he continued, "I think it's time for a few explanations . . ."

Jay started to tell him about Laurie Peters's diamond, the broken gumball machines, the sinister fat man, and all the rest of it. Dottie didn't really listen. She had heard it all the night before. In fact, a few of the key points were hers.

She looked around. Lee and T.J. had managed to clean off most of the mashed fruits and vegetables. Now they were holding out their hands, trying to help up the lady with the pearl necklace. She didn't seem to trust them. Once she got on her feet again, she glared at the two boys, moved away, and started to brush herself off. Now and then she glanced over at them as if she expected them to rush her once again.

Jimmy was still holding the flap shut in the side of the truck. And across the street, Junior was just coming out of Glover's Department Store. *Too bad for him,* thought Dottie. He had missed all the excitement!

Not quite *all* the excitement. Suddenly the rear door of the truck crashed open. Mr. Blackbird stood in the opening, very red in the face, and shook his fist at Jimmy.

"You, young man," he shouted. "Do you have any idea what you have done? You just ruined our shot! Didn't I warn you to stay out of our way?" He started to climb down from the truck.

Phil went over to meet him. "Excuse me," the Chief said in a no-nonsense voice. "Would you mind telling me what is going on here?"

The kids gathered around. Let Mr. Blackbird try to talk his way out of this fix!

"Certainly, sir," he answered pleasantly. "My name is Sidney Blackbird. Let me give you my card."

Blackbird reached inside his suit jacket. "Look out!" Jay cried. "He's pulling a gun!" He rushed forward to grab the man's arm.

"Hold it, son," Phil said, blocking him. "I'll handle this."

"A gun?" Blackbird said, blinking with surprise. "Why on earth would I have a gun? Really, sir, the children of your town have wonderful imaginations. As a rule, I like a child with imagination, but sometimes—"

He pulled his hand from his coat, opened his wallet, and handed Phil a card. "Sidney Blackbird," Phil read. "Producer, *Peek-a-Boo, It's You*." He looked up. "You mean the TV show?" he demanded.

"Quite right," Blackbird replied.

The kids looked at each other. They had watched the show a few times. The gimmick was simple. People found themselves in silly situations, and hidden cameras taped how they acted. Sometimes it was pretty funny.

"Let me get this straight," Phil said. "You're here in Dozerville filming for your show?"

"Exactly, sir. We've been in your town for a week. My staff arranged with the proprietors of several stores to place our gumball machines outside local candy shops. They contain what appear to be valuable pieces of jewelry. Our object, of course, is to see how ordinary people react when they receive a pearl necklace or a ruby ring from a gumball machine."

Phil started to laugh. "Sorry, Mr. Black-

bird," he said. "But these scamps of mine had you figured for the boss of a gang of international jewel thieves."

Blackbird gave him a cold smile. "Indeed?" he said. "Very amusing. What I do not find amusing is that they ruined my shot. Worse, that young man"—he pointed to Jimmy—"may well have damaged our lens when he slammed the flap down on it."

From the back of the truck, the cameraman said, "It didn't help my face, either." He laughed as he rubbed at the red spot on his cheek.

Jay looked around. The whole crowd seemed to find the situation funny. Even Junior was looking at the kids with a nasty grin on his face. No question about it, they had just made fools of themselves.

"Kids?" Phil said. "You go wait in the car while I try to straighten this mess out."

"Right, Chief," Jay replied. "Come on, you guys."

Once inside the old station wagon, they all started to talk at once. "I don't get it," T.J. declared, pounding his knee with his fist. "It all made so much sense!"

"Not really," Dottie said quietly. "Why would real jewel thieves put their loot someplace where anyone, like Laurie, could find it? We never figured that out."

"You know what our mistake was?" asked Jay. "We were too eager to find a case to solve. And once we thought we'd found one, we were too eager to solve it."

"Yeah," Jimmy said sadly. "You know, before the Klinks took us in, we would have done almost anything to get someone to notice us, to think we counted for something. That's why it was so great, getting together with all of you guys and solving real mysteries. It made me feel really special. But now, instead, everybody's laughing at us. They think we're fools."

"Wow," T.J. interrupted, "look at that guy the Chief is talking to now. He looks mad enough to spit nails!"

"Who is he?" asked Lee.

"That's Mr. Arnold," Jimmy replied. "And I bet it means more trouble for us."

"We'll know in a minute," said Jay. "Here comes the Chief."

Phil Klink leaned his arm on the side of the car and put his head in through the window. "You kids have a lot of luck," he said.

"Uh-huh," said Jimmy. "Mostly bad."

"Nope," the Chief replied. "First of all, the camera and lens are okay."

Jay sighed with relief. He had been trying to work out how many years' allowance they would have to give up to replace an expensive lens.

Phil continued. "Once Mr. Blackbird found that out, he calmed down a lot. In fact, you could say that we're getting along pretty well. He even invited me to watch his next shoot, at three o'clock at Dandy Candy."

"Aw," T.J. began.

"And," the Chief said with a grin, "he agreed to let you rascals come, too, if you promise to behave yourselves. I think the idea that you thought he was the mastermind of a gang of jewel thieves kind of tickled him."

All the kids cheered. Maybe they hadn't managed to solve a big mystery, but at least they were going to get to watch a big TV show being made.

"I'd better get back," Phil added, straightening up. "Bob Arnold just told me that someone picked his pocket a few minutes ago while he was shopping at Glover's. I may be retired from the force, but a lot of people still think I'm the law around here."

As Phil walked away, T.J. exclaimed, "A real *Peek-a-Boo* episode, filmed right here in Dozerville—it's hard to believe. I can't wait to see it!"

"Just a second," said Dottie. "The Chief said his friend was robbed just a little while ago in Glover's, didn't he?"

"That's right," Jay replied. "Why?"

"You know the way the pickpocket has

kept turning up near us while we were on this case?'' Dottie continued. ''It can't all be coincidence. I think he's someone connected with the *Peek-a-Boo* show.''

''He can't be,'' Jay said flatly. ''The pick-pocketing started before they got here.''

''Yeah,'' said Jimmy. ''And the whole bunch of them were inside the truck when Mr. Arnold's wallet was stolen.''

Dottie smiled triumphantly. ''Not the *whole* bunch. Guess who I saw coming out of Glover's right in the middle of all the excitement? Junior, that's who. Maybe we didn't uncover a big ring of jewel thieves, the way we thought. But I'll bet we've just tracked down the town pickpocket!''

C·H·A·P·T·E·R
10

*J*immy snapped his notebook shut. "That's it," he said. "A lot of the robberies happened near a candy store we've investigated. And all those stores have gumball machines that Junior takes care of."

"And at least two times, they happened while he was right on the scene," Dottie added. "He's the one."

"Now wait a minute," said Jay. "Last time we jumped to conclusions without really building a case, what happened?"

"We looked like total jerks," T.J. replied.

"Right," Lee said.

"So this time we don't make that mistake," Jay continued. "We find evidence, we question witnesses—"

"We beat the bushes," Lee said.

"We turn over every leaf," T.J. added.

"We scour the pots and pans," said Dottie. "But if we're going to do all that before the shoot at three o'clock, we'd better get moving."

"Great," Jay said, "but moving *where*? Unless we have a plan, we're just spinning our wheels."

Jimmy tapped his notebook. "I say we go back to every spot the pickpocket struck and find out exactly when it happened. Then we check to see if there's a candy store nearby. If there is, we find out when Junior comes around to refill the vending machines. Make sense?"

"Makes sense," Jay agreed. "We'll divide up the list and meet at Dandy Candy as soon as we're done."

Dottie was the first one to get to the meeting point. The familiar truck was parked across the sidewalk from Dandy Candy. She knew without looking that the third gumball machine was now working and that Mr. Blackbird and his film crew were waiting inside the truck to film anyone who put money in it. She stayed on the opposite side of the street, out of the way, and waited for the others to arrive.

T.J. was next. He came riding up wearing a French beret and a billowy white smock with paint stains all over it. Jimmy was not far behind him. A couple of minutes later, Lee and Jay arrived together.

"Well?" Jay demanded. "What have we got?"

"It all checks," Dottie reported. "Junior was around every time the pickpocket struck."

"Same here," said T.J.

"I couldn't pin them all down," Jimmy said, "but the ones I could, he was around." Lee nodded in agreement.

"So it all adds up," Jay said. "Still, it could be coincidence. We don't really have anything linking him directly to the thefts. What we need is to catch him red-handed."

"Look," Lee said excitedly. "Mr. Blackbird just caught someone!"

They looked across the street. A high-school student was standing in front of the gumball machines, staring open-mouthed at something in his hand. It wasn't hard to guess what it was—a valuable-looking gem. After a couple of minutes, Mr. Blackbird came out of the truck and went over to talk to the student. The Chief joined them, and the three laughed together.

"Don't look now," Dottie said softly. "But Junior just went into the Coffee Stop. I want to see what he's doing in there."

"I'm coming with you," said Jay. "You guys wait here."

Jay and Dottie ran across the street and

looked through the window of the cafe. Junior's jacket made him easy to spot. He seemed to be hanging around, waiting for a spot at the lunch counter.

Dottie gasped. "Did you see that?" she demanded. "He took that lady's wallet right out of her purse!"

Jay raised his camera and snapped a picture through the glass. "Too late," he said. "But that gives me an idea. Listen, Dottie, here's what we'll do . . . ."

Dottie shaded her eyes and gazed into the gloomy interior of the truck. There were racks of electronic equipment on either side. An elaborate-looking video camera on a tripod was aimed at a little hole in the side of the truck.

The cameraman was sitting, reading a magazine. "Hi," Dottie said.

"Hi, kid," the man replied.

"My name's Dottie."

The man grinned. "Hi, Dottie," he said. "My name's Hank. You need something?"

"Well . . . would you show me how the camera works? I'm very interested in cameras."

He dropped his magazine on the floor and came over to give her a hand. "Sure," he said. "Come on up."

He flipped a few switches and showed her

where the viewfinder was. There, inside a little tube, was what looked like a tiny TV screen.

"Now this," Hank said, "is what's called a zoom lens. When you push this button, the picture zooms in on whatever you're pointing the camera at."

"Oh, look," Dottie exclaimed. "There are my brothers. They're acting really silly. Can we take their picture?"

"Sure," he replied. "Why not?" He threw a couple more switches and said, "Tape's rolling."

With Hank's help, Dottie focused the camera on Jay, Jimmy, Lee, and T.J. They were horsing around directly in front of the big window of the Coffee Stop. On the other side of the window, Dottie could see some of the customers waiting near the cash register to pay. One of them was Junior.

She pressed the zoom button, just the way Hank had shown her. Suddenly Junior filled the viewfinder. He was holding a newspaper, and his right hand was reaching into the purse of the woman ahead of him in line. When it reappeared, it was holding a wallet.

"What the—!" Hank exclaimed. "Did you see that!"

"I sure did," Dottie replied. "Don't let anything happen to that tape!"

She ran to the back of the truck, leaned out, and waved to Jay and the others. Jay waved back, then ran over to where the Chief was standing, talking with Mr. Blackbird.

A few minutes later, when Junior walked out the door of the Coffee Stop, he found Phil Klink, Mr. Blackbird, and the five Clues Kids waiting for him.

Dottie looked up and gave him one of her sweetest smiles. "Peek-a-boo," she said. "We saw you!"

It was Sunday morning at the Klink house. The whole crowd was in the kitchen. Laurie Peters had come over to retrieve her fake diamond. Snoop was hanging around, wagging his tail, hoping to get a few scraps from the table. And Prowler sat curled up on top of the refrigerator, watching all the action.

The kids had just finished explaining how they had figured out that Junior was the pickpocket. Phil Klink looked up from his griddle full of pancakes and said, "I'm impressed. And I'll tell you who is even more impressed— Sidney Blackbird. He told me that the idea of capturing Junior on tape, in the act of stealing a wallet, was brilliant."

Jay laughed. "It's just like his show," he said. "That's why he thinks it's brilliant."

"Maybe so," Phil said with a grin. "In any

case, he's planning to do a special bit about it on the show. You kids are going to get nationwide exposure."

"Wow," they exclaimed.

"You're going to be famous," Laurie said. "Imagine—five ordinary kids from Dozerville, famous!"

"Hold it," said Jimmy. "What's this 'ordinary' stuff?"

"Coast-to-coast TV," T.J. moaned. "And I didn't even have time to put on a disguise!"

Dottie patted his arm. "That's okay, this way people will know it's you," she said. "You can wear a disguise next time."

From the far end of the table, Patty Klink said, "I'd like one of you kids to disguise yourself as an orange squeezer. There's not nearly enough juice, and my arm is getting tired."

Jimmy sprang up and took over the chore.

"That's better," Patty said, falling into a chair.

"It's so wonderful that you stopped the pickpocket," Laurie exclaimed. "Now Mommy and I can go shopping without fear."

Dottie looked over at Lee and rolled her eyes.

Patty sighed. "I can't wait to see what Tabby Lloyd writes about you kids in tomorrow's paper," she said. "I'm sure she'll be very complimentary."

"Great," Jay said. "That's just the kind of boost the Clues Kids detective agency needs. With so much publicity, our next case—"

Phil Klink interrupted him. "Your next case can wait," he said. "Right now, what I need to know is, who gets this first stack of flapjacks?"

In an instant, the Chief was surrounded, and five plates were thrust in his face.

"Be careful what you ask," Mrs. Klink said with a smile. Everyone burst out laughing.

Another typical Sunday morning in Dozerville.

But this particular morning, and many others, are safer now, thanks to a band of relentless pursuers of evildoers. Five children seeking truth, justice, and a second helping of flapjacks. Five children—who prefer to be known as the Clues Kids.